# Flying Free

# Corey's Underground Railroad Diary

· Book Two ·

## by Sharon Dennis Wyeth

Scholastic Inc.  New York

# Amherstburg, Canada
## 1858

## June 16, 1858

My name is Corey Birdsong. Me and my family are in Canada, in a town called Amherstburg. I ask Daddy how to spell it.

We are staying in Nazrey AME Church. The church has shiny floors and a pea-anno! The preacher of the church is Reverend Binga.

Kind people here give us food.

## Same Day, Later On

We used to live in Kentucky, but we ran away. The Underground Railroad helped us. We ran away 'cause we wanted to be free.

While we were running, slave catchers

chased us. We were afraid. We were afraid to stand still on one spot. Even when we reached Ohio, we had to keep running.

We hid in a boat called the *Pearl*. We crossed a lake and sailed on a river. Then we walked onto the land of Canada. Our jurney was over!

My baby sister Star was smiling.

Daddy looked at the sky and laffed. But Mama got on her knees and started crying.

"We are free!" Daddy say.

"A home, at last!" say Mama.

I look around me. Sun shines on the water! Big trees planted along the road! Crops comin' up across the way!

In Canada, I stand on one spot and I do not feel afraid.

## Later

Mama say I must rest, but I tell her that I cannot rest yet. I did not write the part about the stagecooch.

When we got off the boat, a stagecooch was waiting. A man named Mr. Foster was the driver. He had come to fetch us and take us to the church. The horses rode along the river like the wind.

Mr. Foster owns the stagecooch himself! He told us that he also owns a livery stable. A person of color can make a fine life in Amherstburg. People of color built Nazrey AME Church.

Mama is asleep and so are Star and Daddy. Now, I am falling asleep, too. My family and I had a great jurney. That jurney wore us out.

June 20, 1858

Today is Sunday, and we met a pack of people. They brought us chicken and cakes and such! I ate until my stomach felt like bustin'.

Reverend Binga prayed to the Lord to bless Roland and Angel Birdsong, my daddy and mama. Then he asked the Lord to bless the nine-year-old boy named Corey. (That's me!) Then he asked the Lord to bless the baby named Star, who is seven weeks old.

When the preaching was done, all the people opened their arms to us. Plenty of them had run away from slavery also.

"Welcome, Birdsong family," they say. "You don't have to hide no more."

## Same Day, Later On

Mama sings to Star.

"Oh, don't you want to go to the Promised Land?

That Promised Land ever, where all is peace . . ."

"What is the Promised Land you sing about?" I ask her.

"The Promised Land is a place where we can be safe," Mama say. "A place where we can make our own life."

"Is the Promised Land Canada?" I ask. "Is the Promised Land Amherstburg?"

Mama smiles. "Yes, Corey. I think it might be."

June 26, 1858

Daddy and Mama are looking for work. I watch over Star. I carry Star on my back like a papoose. We walk to the river. We walk to the fort and see the red coat soljers!

Some of the soljers are men of color. I could not take my eyes off them. In Kentucky or Ohio, I never saw a soljer who is my own color.

We walk in the town and see the shops. The shops have clocks and big loaves of bread and cloth and feed for the horses. We pass by Mr. Foster's livery stable and he says good day to us. We meet two of Mr. Foster's friends, a man named Mr. Thurman and a girl named Gwen. Mr. Thurman shook my hand, and Gwen held Star. I am certain that I also saw the Thurmans at church. Gwen wears a bow ribbon.

How good it is to walk where I please!

June 27, 1858

Yesterday I met Mr. Thurman and today I met his wife, Mrs. Thurman. Mrs. Thurman came with Gwen to Nazrey Church to visit the cemetery. Mrs. Thurman's sister is buried in the cemetery at Nazrey. Mrs. Thurman's sister is Gwen's mother. That means that Mr. and Mrs. Thurman are Gwen's uncle and aunt.

After they visited the cemetery, Gwen and Mrs. Thurman came inside the church to say good day to us. Mrs. Thurman gave Mama a big bunch of cornflowers.

Then Gwen and I went for a walk up the road. On our walk, we passed by the schoolhouse! I looked in the windows and saw the desks. The school is empty now, but it will start up again in the fall.

Gwen asked if I will be going. I told her that I hope so. I have never been to school. My

father and mother have taught me everything I know.

## Same Day, Later On

Here are the names of our new friends in Amherstburg:

Gwen Thurman
Mr. Foster (of Foster's Stagecooch and Livery Stable)
Reverend and Mrs. Binga (of Nazrey AME Church)
Mr. and Mrs. Thurman (Gwen's uncle and aunt)

## June 28, 1858

Today I walked to the woods. So many birds! All colors of birds, flying every which-

a-way! Many more birds than in Kentucky, seems to me. Singing plenty of songs! I think that Star liked them also. She did not cry a bit, when all those birds were flying around. Saw a pretty purpel bird, which I had never seen. Birds have always been one of my best things.

## June 29, 1858

Daddy has work! He will work in the Navvy Yard. In the Navvy Yard, there is work for a blacksmith.

Mama has work! She is sewing shirts for people in town! Mama is a fine scamstress. Her stittches are small and even. When we lived in Kentucky, Mama did not get paid for her work. Now she will get paid.

## Same Day, Later On

Mrs. Binga brought us 'taters and beans from her garden. I mashed the 'taters for Mama.

After supper I tell Daddy about the purpel bird. Daddy asks me what the bird's song sounds like. The purpel bird has a sweet chirrup. I try to make the song, but it is too hard for me.

## Later

Daddy read my book. He gave me these new spelling words.

PIANO
JOURNEY
LAUGHED
STAGECOACH
SOLDIERS

PURPLE
NAVY
STITCHES
POTATOES

Daddy told me to go back to the places where I spelled these words in the wrong way. He wants me to spell them correctly. I did that, except I did not change the word 'taters.

I do not call them potatoes. I call them 'taters. So, that is the way I am going to spell them. This is my book and I will spell 'taters the way I please.

**June 30, 1858**

Daddy took me with him to the Navy Yard. Plenty of things for ships there. Daddy be fixing the big chains. I look over the water and see land. On the land there is a lighthouse.

"Is that Ohio?" I ask Daddy.

"No," says Daddy. "That is an island by the name of Bois Blanc."

"Where is Ohio?" I ask.

"On the other side of the island," Daddy says. "Across the river are Ohio and Michigan. If you cross where the river is most narrow, you will come to Michigan. So, the States are not too far away."

## Same Day, Later On

In the States I had to hide, so that the slave catchers wouldn't catch me. In Canada I don't have to hide. In the States I was afraid. In Canada I am not afraid. Yet Daddy says that the States are not too far away. Maybe I am wrong to not be afraid.

## July 1, 1858

Last night I had a dreem. In my dreem I was running with my best friend, Mingo. We were in Kentucky and dogs were chasing us.

This was only a dreem. Mingo did not run away with me. Mingo stayed behind in Kentucky. He is still a slave on the Hart place.

When I remember Mingo, I am sad.


## Same Day, Later On

Late in the day, Mama took me and Star to the bakery. The bakery is owned by Mr. and Mrs. McCurdy. We have met the McCurdys in church. The bread smells delicious in their bakery!

Mama has made Mr. McCurdy a new shirt. Mama gave the shirt to Mrs. McCurdy. Then Mrs. McCurdy gave Mama two loaves of bread for our family to eat. Mama say she will come again for more bread.

For one new shirt, Mrs. McCurdy will give Mama all the bread we need for the next two weeks.

## July 5, 1858

Much has happened. I have work! I also have a new friend. His name is George. I cannot write in my book this minute. I am too buzy!

## July 6, 1858

I work for Reverend Binga. I pick beans on his farm. I pick squash and 'taters. I pick all the vejedables that grow there. The Binga place is a few miles away from where my family and I live at Nazrey Church. Mama say it worries her to have me working so far off. She wants to keep an eye on me. Daddy tells her not to worry.

I will write about my new friend George tomorrow. My eyes are closing.


## July 7, 1858

My new friend is named George Davis. He is eleven years old. George works with me on the Binga farm. George picks vejedables faster than lightneeng.

George told me about his family. They used to live in Verginia. They ran away from Verginia when George was a baby.

George say his grandmother and his uncle are still in Verginia. They are slaves. George and his mother, father, and brother are saving money. Someday they will buy freedom for George's uncle and grandmother.

George's father is a mate on a ferryboat.

George's mother raises chickens. They also have a cow.

## Same Day, Later On

I told George about Mingo. How Mingo got whipped for tasting ol' Hart's peaches. Mingo didn't run away, because he wanted to stay with Aunt Queen. Aunt Queen raised Mingo. Aunt Queen is still on ol' Hart's place. So is Daddy's friend Charles. Charles ran away like we did, but he got caught.

I do not want to think about my days in Kentucky, but I cannot help thinking about my friends.

Reverend Binga gave me plenty of vejedables to take home. Those vejedables are my pay. Daddy is proud of me.

I cut some nice corn tassels for Mama. She wants to dry the corn silk to make a doll for Star.

**July 8, 1858**

Today on our way home, George and I looked at birds. So many different kinds of ducks in Canada. We saw the purple birds I like. George said the purple birds are called purple martins.

I did my birdcalls for George. I did the robin and the blue jay and the crow and the whip-poor-will. My new friend was surprised.

"Don't be surprised," I told him. "That is why my last name is Birdsong. My friend Aunt Queen gave me that name, when I did my birdcalls down in Kentucky."


**Same Day, Later On**

Daddy is making good wages at the Navy Yard. Over two dollars a day! He is saving so we can buy our own farm. Mama cannot believe it.

"Our own farm!" This is like a dreem to us, having our own place someday. We are still living in the Nazrey Church, after all. Every Sunday we roll up our things and put them away in a corner. Then Nazrey Church is looking like a church again and not somebody's home.

Reverend Binga told Mama that she could try to play the piano. Mama pressed down on the keys and the sound was delightful.

## July 10, 1858

This evening Daddy read my book. He gave me some spelling words. He say, "You are a good writer, Corey. Keep this book with you forever. You are telling the Birdsong family story."

DIFFERENT
DREAM
BUSY

VEGETABLES
LIGHTNING
VIRGINIA

## July 15, 1858

Today I did not work for Reverend Binga.
Today I worked in Mr. Foster's livery stable. I
fed and groomed the horses. I also helped Mr.
Foster take the mailbag off the stagecoach. I
took the mailbag to the post office. I had never
been inside of a post office before. People get
letters there. They also send them.

## Same Day, Later On

Maybe I will send a letter to Mingo! Only,
Mingo might not be able to read it. Before I
left, I was teaching him how to write. But all
he could write was his name.

July 16, 1858

I worked in town again today. I cared for Mr. Foster's horses and then I went to the post office. I asked the man who works in the post office if I can sweep up for him. His name is Mr. Peche. He is a white man, but he treated me nicely. I swept up for Mr. Peche and he gave me a coin. I know I should save that coin, but I spent some on a peppermint stick. First time in my life that I bought something in a sweet shop. That was some sweet candy! The rest of my pay I will give to Mama.

## Same Day, Later On

I almost forgot to write down something very essciting. In town today I heard the town crier. He is a man that holds a scroll of paper and reads out the news. He has a loud voice.

He is a colored man! Made me proud to see a man of color having this important post. Town crier! He told about some doin's at the fort. The red coat soldiers were listening up. He told about some folks getting married. Everybody listened to him. He is the town crier! His name is Mr. Adams. The whole town must listen to him!

**July 18, 1858**

Today after church, George and I went swimming. Some other boys went along with us. The girls went berry picking. We had a high time swimming in the river. Saw me a heron bird. One of George's friends, Swenson, was talkin' about Frederick Douglass.

"I know who Mr. Douglass is," I say. "I read his newspaper, *The North Star*."

"Frederick Douglass was in a town not far

from here," Swenson say. "He was there with John Brown and Harriet Tubman. No more than a few weeks ago. I went to see them!"

"Wish I could have seen them," I say.

"John Brown said that we must fight to free the slaves. We got to go back and help the slaves to rise up," say Swenson.

This abolitionist talk reminds me of my days running away on the Underground Railroad. If it were not for the Underground Railroad's help, I would not be in Canada.

## Same Day, Later On

That talk about rising up against slavery is still on my mind. I cannot help but to think about Mingo. How can I help him rise up?

Here are names of more folks in Amherstburg:

George Davis (friend who picks vegetables
   faster than lightning)
Swenson (he saw Frederick Douglass)
Mr. and Mrs. McCurdy (McCurdy's Bakery)
Mr. Adams (town crier)
Mr. Peche (postmaster)


## July 23, 1858

Mama made me a new shirt. It is blue.
Mama cut the red cloth from my old shirt into
small pieces. She will sew the pieces into a
quilt she is making. On Sunday I will wear my
fine new shirt to church.


## July 26, 1858

Daddy met a giant! He is really a very tall
and strong man. He is a blacksmith and he has

his own blacksmith shop. Everybody in town calls him Giant! The Malagasy Giant! The Malagasy Giant asked Daddy to work for him in his blacksmith shop.

Behind the blacksmith shop there is a small house. This small house is next to the one where the Giant lives with his wife. Daddy says that the Birdsong family is going to move out of Nazrey Church. We will live in the small house on the Giant's land. The rent for the house will come out of Daddy's wages.

Nazrey Church has been a good home.


July 27, 1858

We moved into the small house on the Malagasy Giant's land. The Giant's real name is Mr. Bentley. Mrs. Bentley gave Mama quilts for our beds. She gave Star a baby dress. She gave me some breeches. Then I fed Mrs. Bentley's chickens for her. After that I put clean straw in the matteresses.

Mama made vegetable soup on the woodstove. I gathered the wood for her and made the fire. Daddy say he smelled that good soup all the way over at the forge.

Daddy says the grace. "Thank you for the soup, Lord. Thank you for these four walls."

## July 28, 1858

Today I heard the town crier telling about a big celebrashun! A big celebrashun for Emancipashun Day! I asked George to tell me about it.

"This day will be the finest in my life!" George says. "And it is coming soon! There will be a big perade, drumming, and all kinds of fine food. This celebrashun is for the freedom of the black people in Canada."

Mama and Daddy are also excited. I will wear my new shirt, and Star will wear the baby dress that Mrs. Bentley gave to Mama. Daddy say he will ride Mr. Foster's team in the buggy race!

## Same Day, Later On

I cannot get the celebrashun out of my mind. All kinds of folks will be there. Swenson and the boys I met with George will be there. Gwen also. The celebrashun will be at a grove. Might be I will fish some. Might be that I will be in some races.

July 29, 1858

I had another dream about Mingo. Mingo and I were playing marbles. Then Young Bob Hart, ol' Hart's son, played with us also.

I remember that Young Bob Hart tried to treat me and Mingo nice. Young Bob was trying, but his father was hard-hearted. Anyone who is a masser must be hard-hearted. I think so.


July 30, 1858

Daddy read my book today. Here are some spelling words.

MATTRESSES
EMANCIPATION
CELEBRATION
PARADE

**Same Day, Later On**

To tell the truth, Daddy is giving me too many spelling words. He tells me to learn them soon as I can. Though I do like to spell a heap of words, tonight I do not feel like it.

Daddy asked me about Mingo. "Do you miss Mingo, Corey?"

I tell him. "Yes, sir. I do. Can we do something to get Mingo free like we are?"

Daddy shakes his head. "I don't know how we can at the moment. We must settle ourselves first."


**July 31, 1858**

Emancipation Day!

My family and I walked to the green near the fort. I could hear the drums! I started to run. All our friends from the church were gathered and many more people. Some had buggies loaded up with food. Mr. Thurman brought his pig in a wagon.

I found George in the crowd. The parade started. The most wonderful sight was a group of colored soldiers in red coats!

The whole crowd began marching. George and I marched behind the drummer. We marched to the grove.

At the grove, the real fun started. A fellow stood on some stilts and jugled six balls in the air!

Daddy drove Mr. Foster's team in the buggy race and he won! His prize was some sugar.

George and I ran in the three-legged race.

Then fiddlers began to play and the dancing started. Mama and Daddy cut a fine figure. I put Star on my shoulders to watch them.

## Same Day, Later On

Here are some other things that happened.

Mr. Thurman's pig won the prize for being the fattest.

Some of the ladies put on a fashion show. Gwen was in that part, wearing a fancy bonnet.

There was also a showing of quilts. Mrs. Bentley showed off three that she had made. Mama truly admired them.

I was in the tug of war! My shirt got muddy, but then I went swimming.

I hope that I have not left out anything. I had no time for fishing.

The second day of the celebration is tomorrow.

## August 1, 1858

Early this morning, we went back to the grove. Reverend Binga was preaching a sunrise service. The sun was just coming up when he started the preaching. He said we were one big family. He said we should not forget the ones we left behind. Then everyone sang.

"Shall we meet beyond the river?

Shall we meet beyond the river, when the stormy voyage is over?"

After the service, dinner was laid out. One hundred pies! Biscuits, greens, corn, ham, chicken, pickles, sweet 'taters, 'tater salad! Mrs. Thurman and Gwen made strawberry ice cream. I helped turn the crank on the ice cream maker. Today Gwen did not have on that bonnet. I am glad. That bonnet might be fancy, but it is silly looking. Instead she wore a yella bow ribbon.

### Same Day, Later On

After dinner, there was more preaching. George's big brother say he wants to be bapptized. So Reverend Binga took him to the stream and pushed him under, then brought him back up again.

After that, another tug of war and more foot races.

Somebody started up bird calling. I got in on that. George says my whip-poor-will call is the best he has heard.

We walked back home when the sun was going down. We were taking our time.

It is surely good to be free.

### August 8, 1858

Today is my birthday. I am ten years old. Daddy gave me a whitteling knife. And Mama made a blackberry cake! Mama used some of the sugar that Daddy won in the buggy race.

There was sugar inside of the cake and sugar on top. My mouth was watering. But before I could get a taste, Mama made me take two big slices to the Malagasy Giant and Mrs. Bentley. Then Mr. Foster came down the road. So Mama gave two big pieces to him. Reverend and Mrs. Binga were still at the church, so Daddy carried some of my cake over to them.

Finally, Mama cut some for us! That cake was tasty! Star is too young to eat cake. But Star grabbed a bit from my piece and put it in her hair.

I was hoping to get a second slice, but George came by. So we gave him the last of it. All the same, it was good.

## Same Day, Later On

I took some paper from my book and wrote a letter to Mingo. I hope he will understand the meaning of what I wrote.

Mingo ➶★ Amherstburg. Your friend, C.

He has one friend whose name is Birdsong.


## August 9, 1858

Today I went to the post office and asked Mr. Peche for an envelope. I swept up the place, so he gave me one. I was fixing to mail Mingo's letter. But I did not want to be so stupid as to write the address of Ol' Hart's Farm on the outside. Ol' Hart would get that letter and keep it himself, I am certain. So I wrote the name of our friend in town, a free colored man who is a blacksmith. His name is Mr.

Babe Jameson. He will give Mingo that letter on the sly, so that Masser Hart won't know about it.

I gave Mr. Peche the envelope with Mingo's letter in it. He said that he will make certain that it is posted.

I also met Mr. Peche's son today. He looks to be my age. I did not know how he would treat me, since he is a white boy. But he is friendly, just like his father. His name is Pierre. Pierre Peche. His hair is yella.


**August 11, 1858**

Good news! Mr. Thurman took Mama, Daddy, Star, and me out to his place today. Mr. Thurman has a stone quary. More important, he has lots of land. He has offered to sell our family a parcel. Mr. Thurman will give us a very good price. We can pay for the land over time. Mr. and Mrs. Thurman want us to be their naybers. I look out at those akers of land. Is this a dream? Will the Birdsongs someday be landowners? Daddy and Mama say they will buy that land or break their back trying.

When we rode back by the Thurman house, I saw Gwen on the porch. Someday Gwen and I will be naybers.

## August 15, 1858

Today in church, we met a new family. They came to town only last night. They have come all the way from Alabama! The family's name is Johnston. They will be living for a spell in Nazrey Church, just as our family did.

Mrs. Johnston looked mighty poorly. Mr. Johnston's feet were cut up. They have a young boy named Sammy. His eyes look afraid.

Maybe he thinks that the catchers are still after him. During church, Mrs. Johnston was crying. When the service was over, we opened our arms to them.

"Welcome, Johnston family," everyone said. "You don't have to run no more."

## Same Day, Later On

Mama say that Mrs. Johnston is tore up inside over the loss of her baby. The baby was a girl, and while the family was running north, the baby girl died. Made me sad myself to hear that.

Daddy is taking an iron pot over to the church for the Johnstons to cook in. I am gathering some kindling for them. Mama has made squirrel stew today. There is enough to share, so Mama will put some stew in that iron pot. Then the Johnstons can have stew for dinner.

**August 16, 1858**

I helped Daddy at the forge today. We were shoeing a horse for Mr. Foster. Then Daddy and I took a walk on the river. We came on some fine looking ducks. We saw a flock of geese in the sky, flying south.

"I read your book last night, son," say Daddy.

"Did you find me spelling words?" I asked him.

Daddy nods his head. "I also learned that you wrote a letter to Mingo."

"Yes, sir," I said.

Daddy put his arm on my shoulder. "That is not safe, son," he say. "Ol' Hart might get wind of where we are. He might find that letter that you sent to Mingo."

"Ol' Hart can't hurt us now," I tell Daddy.

"Ol' Hart might hurt us still, Corey," Daddy say. He points across the river at the island. "Slave catchers wait on that island, trying to get folks like us. They think if they bide their time, they can snatch us and take us back south."

**Same Day, Later On**

What Daddy told me made me afraid. It also surprised me.

"We are free people now," I told him. "We are living in Canada. There is no law here that says we are slaves."

"That's true," Daddy say. "But those catchers will try to get us if they can. They will get well paid if they take one of us back. Be careful, Corey."

Though I am worried, I am not sorry that I wrote my letter to Mingo.

**August 17, 1858**

Spelling Words


JUGGLED

YELLOW

BAPTIZED

WHITTLING

QUARRY

ACRES

NEIGHBOR


**August 18, 1858**

We picked melons at Reverend Binga's farm today. He gave me several to take home.

When we walk back into town, George and I pass by the schoolhouse. George asked me if I was going to school next week. To go to school has always been one of my dreams.

"Mrs. Cary visited our school last year," George boasted.

"Who is she?" I ask.

"A smart colored lady who has her own newspaper. The paper is called the *Provincial Freeman*," said George.

## August 19, 1858

This is the worst day of my life. I lost my baby sister.

I took Star to the river. I wanted to show her the ducks. A white man came up in his wagon. He asked me if I wanted a ride. I told him that I didn't need a ride. Then he asked me if I was born in Amherstburg. I told him that I was born in Kentucky and that my sister was born in Ohio. Then he asked me to get up into his wagon. He needed help moving some sacks. He said that he would pay me if I helped him.

I laid Star beneath a tree and climbed into the wagon. I shifted the sacks around for the man. But he didn't pay me. Before I know what is happening, he starts driving off. "Sit down!" he yells at me.

But I didn't sit down. I jumped off. I jumped off the wagon and began running. The man yelled for me to come back, but I didn't. I was afraid.

I did not stop running until I got into town. That is when I remembered my baby sister. I had left her under the tree! I ran back as fast as I could, but Star was gone!

## Same Day, Later On

What a long day! The whole town was out looking for Star. Mr. Adams, the town crier, was calling out the news that Star was missing. He was calling it out for all to hear.

Mrs. Binga told Mama that the man in the wagon was probably a slave catcher. He was out looking for some people of color that he could steal. He could take them back in a boat to the States and get paid for them.

I was crying and crying. I looked everywhere along the river. Finally, Mr. Thurman found Star on the side of the road not far from his house. Gwen was with him when the baby was found! They brought Star home. I was never so happy in my life!

Later on, I heard Mama say that the man was more than likely after me. But then I jumped off his wagon. When he found Star, he decided to steal her instead. But the man must have thought twice about it, because Star is too little to work. We will never know the real story. Maybe Star cried so loud that she scared that mean ol' man.

**August 20, 1858**

I asked Mama and Daddy about going to school. Of course I will go to school, Daddy say! Mama has already made me some new blue breeches. She made them as a surprise. Daddy say that he is fixing a cart wheel for the cobbler. So, that cobbler has made me some shoes.


**August 22, 1858**

George brought the *Provincial Freeman* to church today. I showed it to Daddy. There is much in that paper against slavery. Daddy went to a meeting at Mr. Foster's and took me with him. A man named Mr. Osborne was speaking. Mr. Osborne has met John Brown. He told us we must fight against slavery. We are free, but others are not.

## August 23, 1858

Today I went to school! I wore my new shoes and breeches. I have a new slate to write on. I shook the teacher's hand. His name is Mr. John Alexander. His is the smartest person in the world.

## Same Day, Later On

George was at school. So was Gwen. So were Swenson and young Sammy Johnston, who still lives at Nazrey Church.

When Mr. Alexander asked somebody to spell a word, I was the first to answer. That is because I am a double head, I told George after school. "I can read and write. My daddy taught me."

"I think you are a swelled head," George said.

I think that George was jellus.

**Later**

I practiced my handwriting as Mr. Alexander told us to do. I also learned my spelling.

APPLE
AX
AGRICULTURE

Agriculture means farming.

**September 1, 1858**

I do not have time to write as much. I have homework every night. I am learning my numbers, how to add and subtract. George is better at numbers than I am. Now I am the jellus one.

After school I also work. I am apple picking with George at Reverend Binga's. He gives me apples to take home, but he also pays me. I made twenty-five cents today!

The leaves are turning colors. Gwen and I saw a scarlet tanager! The scarlet tanager is Gwen's favorite bird. I can do the tanager's song. It has a song like the robin.

## September 5, 1858

Star wiggles around on her belly. She is also very noisy. Sometimes she sounds like a bird. "Coo-coo." My baby sister keeps us awake with her bird talk!

## September 7, 1858

I went to the post office after school. I saw Pierre Peche. He goes to another school. He looked to see if there was a letter for me, but there wasn't. I keep hoping that I will get some word from Mingo. Pierre told me that he will be on the lookout for my letter.

## September 10, 1858

Mama got a Bible from one of the elders in the church. She asked me to read it for her. Mama likes to listen to me read.

"I would like to learn to read myself," she told me, when I finished.

"I will teach you how, Mama," I promised her.

I showed her how to sound out some words. The quilt that Mama is making is coming

along right well. She is adding pieces of white that look like wings.

**September 13, 1858**

When George and I were walking with Gwen, we saw a hawk. Then we saw an eagle. George asked me to do a birdcall. I did a duck! That made Gwen laugh.

**September 17, 1858**

Today is Mama's birthday. Mrs. Bentley took care of Star and I took Mama to my school.

Mama sat in the back of the room and practiced her letters. She copied the words off the board.

"You are writing well, Mrs. Birdsong," said Mr. Alexander.

"Thank you," said Mama. She smiled at me. "I have a good teacher at home."

On our way home, we picked some corn in the Bentleys' field. Mama will dry some of the husks for Star's doll.

## September 20, 1858

Another family arrived today. They came over on the *Pearl*, just like we did. Mr. Osborne brought them to stay with the Bentleys. Mama sent me over to the Bentleys with two shirts and a shawl. The new family was eating when I came in, but they stopped eating to thank me. Their name is Dennis and they come from Maryland. Tomorrow they will be moving on to another town, where they have family.

## September 21, 1858

I want to be a member of the Underground Railroad. I want to go back to Kentucky and rescue Mingo.

I could go back across the lake on the *Pearl*. I could hide in the woods. I could find the Hart place where I used to be a slave. I could find Mingo and show him the way to Canada.

I asked Daddy about this. He and Mama will not let me go. It is too dangerous, they say. "We will try to find a way of helping Mingo as soon as we can," Daddy promised.

I wish that I was grown up and could decide things on my own. I would go find Mingo in Kentucky today. I would join the Underground Railroad.

## October 3, 1858

We have saved enough money to give Mr. Thurman his first payment for the land! The rest we will pay over time. Also, Daddy will fix carts to help pay the price off. Mr. Thurman uses the carts to carry stones from his quarry.

We are landowners! We will build a log cabin on the land that will be all our own. Daddy said that the work I have done has helped him and Mama. I helped put food on the table. Without my help, he and Mama would not have been able to save up the money.

## October 12, 1858

Daddy and I are clearing our land. We are clearing a spot for the cabin. We are digging out stones. Mama is laying out a spot for the garden. Next year we will grow our own vegetables.

Mama say that one very good thing about our new land is that it is farther from the river. Folks who live farther from the river are safer.

## October 14, 1858

Mr. Alexander gave us some reading that I like very much. Here is some poetry about a bluebird!

*I know the song that the bluebird is singing*
*Out in the apple tree where he is swinging.*
*Brave little fellow! The skies may be dreary —*
*Nothing cares he while his heart is so cheery.*

## October 23, 1858

I swept up for Mr. Peche. Mingo has not answered my letter.

Daddy and I have cleared a right nice plot for the house. George and his father, Mr. Davis, are helping us. So is Mr. Thurman.

Star is cutting a tooth. Mama lets her suck on a piece of hard bread.

## October 24, 1858

Mama is making me a coat. Winter is coming soon. We hear the geese as they fly south. I watch them in the sky. The coat that Mama is making for me will be brown. She will also use some of the scraps for her quilt.

## October 29, 1858

Yesterday we cut trees from Reverend Binga's woods. We brought the logs over to our land. George's father also let us cut trees on the Davis place. They have a wood lot. George helped me and his father and Mr. Thurman and Daddy to take the logs back to our new land.

Mr. Thurman has been helping Daddy to lay a foundation for the cabin. The foundation is made out of stones. We will lay the logs on top of the stone foundation.

## October 30, 1858

Today was the church social. The eating was indoors, but the games and music were on the lawn. My teacher Mr. Alexander played nine pins with George and me! Then Mr.

Foster played the banjo, and the Malagasy Giant did some drumming. Mrs. Thurman wanted to teach the young people a jig. Gwen said she would try, but George and I ran away from that one.

**Same Day, Later On**

After the social, Daddy was talking with Mr. Osborne and the Malagasy Giant. I listened to them in back of the church. Mr. Osborne is thinking of going back south to join up with John Brown.

**November 1, 1858**

Today I saw large white birds flying overhead. The whole sky was filled with them. Their wings made a whistling sound! Gwen and

George say those birds be called whistling swans.

## November 2, 1858

This afternoon I saw the postmaster, Mr. Peche. He was riding up the road in his buggy. I was getting in the kindling for the fire. "I got something for you, Corey Birdsong," he say. "A letter. Come by for it tomorrow."

## Same Day, Later On

That letter must be from Mingo!

## November 3, 1858

After school today I went to the post office. I got my letter. It had my name written on the outside. George and Gwen were waiting for me. We went off by ourselves to open the letter. It is from Mingo! He has written his name on it. MINGO →★

There is a picture of a star. This must be the North Star, same as what I put in my letter to him. This means that Mingo plans to run away from Kentucky. He will follow the North Star, just as my family did. But what town will Mingo run to? Gwen asks. Is your friend Mingo coming here to Amherstburg? George asks. If so, when is he coming?

I tell Gwen and George that they must keep Mingo's letter a secret. But I will tell Mama and Daddy.


## Same Day, Later On

I showed Mingo's letter to Daddy and Mama. They agree that Mingo has run. Daddy says that he will speak with the captain of the *Pearl*. Sometimes he hears news about runaways. Mama says that she hopes that Mingo finds us. She hopes that he will have a safe journey.

### November 4, 1858

I am thinking of Mingo all the time. Maybe the Underground Railroad will help Mingo, like they helped us.

### November 7, 1858

Today in church I prayed for Mingo.

### November 10, 1858

I will not go to school for a while. I must help Daddy with our cabin. The stone

foundation is finished. I help Daddy and Mr. Thurman notch the logs. We lay the logs across the stones. Then we lay the logs across one another. Our neighbors from church will help us. Daddy say we will raise the cabin before the first hard snow.

**November 11, 1858**

I went to school to say hello to Mr. Alexander. He knows that I will not be coming for a while. Mr. Alexander gave me a book to take home with me. In the book is a story to read about a Mr. Audubon and his pictures. It goes like this.

"There is a great naturalist. His name is Mr. Audubon. He wanted to understand the habits of plants and animals. He made up his mind to write a great book about birds. Mr. Audubon could draw and paint beautifully."

Mr. Alexander also gave me some spelling words.

DREARY
CHEERY
SWINGING
AUDUBON
UNDERSTAND
HABITS
BEAUTIFULLY

**November 15, 1858**

Our cabin has four walls! We have been working hard. Every morning we leave our small house on the Giant's place and travel to our own land. Today the Giant himself came to help us. Soon we will lay the cedar planks for the roof.

Daddy and Mr. Thurman built a stone

hearth. Mama lit a fire on it. That is where the stove will be someday. I do miss school, but I like helping out.

The Malagasy Giant say that I handle an ax right well.

## November 20, 1858

Today I heard gunshots in the woods. George was over helping with the cabin. We are putting chinking between the logs. We thought someone must be hunting. Maybe they shot a deer.

Later we walked to the creek on our land. Close by we found a whistling swan. His wing was wounded. A hunter had shot him. I carried the swan back to our cabin. Mama helped me splint his wing. The swan hissed at Star and she cried.

## November 21, 1858

Today after church, we came back to our land. I made a pen next to the creek for my swan. I put straw in it. I gave my swan some corn to eat. He is a beautiful bird.

## November 25, 1858

This morning, we finished the roof on our cabin! We also have a mud chimney. Mrs. Thurman came by with Gwen. They brought apple pie and Mama made coffee. Mr. McCurdy was over today, too, with Mrs. McCurdy. Everyone thinks that the Birdsongs' new cabin is a fine one!

## November 26, 1858

We moved to our new cabin! We have some cedar planks for the table. We have barrels for chairs. We brought our beds with us and the quilts that Mrs. Bentley made.

The Malagasy Giant and Mrs. Bentley helped us move. Then we all said good-bye.

It was sad to say good-bye to them. The Bentleys were like family. But we will see them at church. And of course Daddy still works with the Giant.

At last we have our very own home!

## December 1, 1858

I went back to school today. I have longer to walk from our new home. On the way, I met Gwen up at her house. Then we met George at the Davis place. Then the three of us walked together.

Gwen told me that in school there will be a spelling bee. I have never been in a spelling bee before.

## Same Day, Later On

After school I went to the post office. I saw Pierre Peche. I asked him to look to see if there was another letter for me. There wasn't.

Where is Mingo? Did he get caught?

## December 7, 1858

Today in church I saw the captain of the *Pearl*. I asked him if he had heard anything about Mingo. He told me that he hadn't heard of a runaway by that name.

### December 9, 1858

Swan's wing is mending up. But he still cannot fly. He does walk back and forth to the creek, however. He eats bugs from the creek. Mama says Swan can fend for himself. But I still keep my eye on him. His family has left him. He is all on his own.

### December 11, 1858

Today Mrs. Foster gave Mama a rocking chair! She sits in the chair and rocks Star. When Star goes to sleep, Mama sits in the chair and sews on her quilt.

Tomorrow is the spelling bee.

## December 12, 1858

Gwen won the spelling bee. I almost won. But I could not spell the word jealous. I will never forget that word in my life. I am glad that Gwen won, if I could not. The prize was a book of poetry.

## December 14, 1858

Good news! The captain of the *Pearl* was at church today. He showed Mama and Daddy and me a poster for a runaway. He found the poster in Ohio. The poster was about a runaway named Mingo. This Mingo ran away from the Hart farm in Kentucky! Now we know that our friend is still running! He has not been caught yet! Hurry Mingo, we are waiting!

### December 15, 1858

Last night I had a dream that dogs were chasing Mingo. I remember when dogs chased Mama and me. I hope that dogs are not really chasing Mingo. I hope this is only a dream.

### December 16, 1858

This morning Star woke me up! She was babbling loud as a brook.

### December 17, 1858

I went to work with Daddy today. After he worked at his forge, he showed me a surprise. He has been building a table for Mama. At Christmas we will have a real table to eat on. Not planks laid across four barrels.

Ice floats on the river.

## December 23, 1858

Two more days to Christmas! Daddy's table is finished. He and I will bring it home tomorrow. I had not quite finished the gifts I was making. Today the Malagasy Giant gave me some paint. I have finally finished the gifts I was making.

## December 24, 1858

George, Gwen, and I helped to green the church today. The windows and chairs have ropes of pine on them. The smell is quite fresh. Tomorrow will be my first Christmas as a free person.

## December 25, 1858

There is much to write about Christmas Day. Early in the morning, we woke up and had a special breakfast. Mama fried apples! We had corn bread and coffee. We had ham! We had blueberry jam, a gift to Mama from Mrs. McCurdy. Last night Daddy and I brought home the new table. Mama liked it so much! We ate breakfast at the new table.

Then I gave out my gifts — three small swans that I whittled with my knife. I painted them white. I gave one to each person in my family. Then Mama and Daddy gave me an orange and some marbles. Mama gave Star the doll she made. The doll's body is a dried corncob covered with dried cornhusks. The doll has hair made out of dried corn silk. Mama made a dress for the doll out of some of the scraps from my old red shirt! She made the hat out of cornhusks. On the hat are dried cornflowers. My baby sister loves her new doll!

My orange is very juicy.

I will write more later on.

## Same Day, Later On

After breakfast we went to church. The church was filled with lit candles. Mrs. Binga played hymns on the piano. We sang "Silent Night."

Then came the raffle! Underneath each seat in the church was a raffle ticket. A basket of presents sat waiting at the front of the church. The numbers were drawn out of a hat.

Mrs. Johnston won a coffeepot! Mr. Davis won a new ax.

After the raffle, a present was given to the oldest member of the church. That is old Mrs. McCurdy, Mr. McCurdy's mother. Old Mrs. McCurdy's present was a warm shawl.

Then a present was given to the youngest. The youngest member of the church is Star! Her gift was a doll cradle.

After those gifts were given out, the rest of

us children played Christmas Gift. I got me a bunch of walnuts and some hard candy! Then we all ate a big dinner together with turkey and stuffing. This was the best Christmas of my whole life!

**December 30, 1858**

The river is nearly all frozen over. We can smell in the air that a storm is coming. I put more straw in Swan's pen, so he won't be too cold. There is still running water in the creek, so Swan can catch something to eat there. I want to bring Swan into the house, but Mama and Daddy say that he is a wild thing. Wild things should not come indoors with people. They will forget how to fend for themselves.

## January 1, 1859

I have come down with fever. Mama say I must stay in bed.

## January 3, 1859

For the past two days I felt quite sick. But at last my fever is gone. Mama and Daddy say I must stay indoors, however. My legs are weak when I walk.

I am reading the book that Mr. Alexander gave to me about Mr. Audubon and his bird pictures.

## January 4, 1859

Mama had gone to town to visit the McCurdys. Mrs. McCurdy has the same fever that I had. But she did not get well yet. She is

quite bad off. So Mama has gone to help out Mr. McCurdy in the bakery.

Mama says that I am lucky that my fever went away so quickly. Daddy will not let me go to school as yet, however. He wants to make certain that I am all well. We are mighty glad that Star did not catch it.

## January 5, 1859

Though I feel well, Mama and Daddy will not let me go outdoors still. I miss George and my other friends at school. Mama is still helping the McCurdys. She takes Star with her. Daddy goes to work with the Giant. So I am alone in the house.

**January 6, 1859**

Dear Mama and Daddy,

I hope that you find this letter in my diary. After you left today, Pierre Peche, the postmaster's son, came to our house. He came on his mule. He told me that there was some mail for me. A big box with my name on it. The problem is that the box did not come across on the boat. The river is too froze up. Pierre say that Mr. Peche walked across the river where it is most narrow. He walked across to Michigan to fetch the letters. But the box was too big to carry across.

I am going to town with Pierre on his mule. I think that I should see about this box that has been left across the river. It has the letter "M" written on it! I hope to be home soon.

Corey

## January 9, 1859

My son, Corey Birdsong, walked across the ice to Bois Blanc Island on January 7. He then walked across the Detroit River to Michigan. He found a large box. Inside of the box was his friend Mingo! Though Mingo was almost frozen, he was still alive. Recorded this day by Corey's father, Roland Birdsong.

## January 10, 1859

I am Angel Birdsong, Corey's mother. I am writing in Corey's diary. Corey is very sick. Much sicker than he was before. His fever came back.

Mingo is also poorly. His toes were frozen.

**January 15, 1859**

Get well soon, Corey. Your friend, Gwen Thurman

**January 16, 1859**

Corey's fever has broken at last! My son is still quite weak, however. Roland Birdsong.

**January 20, 1859**

Get well soon, Corey. Mr. and Mrs. Thurman

**January 21, 1859**

I was here. You were sleeping. Hello from your friend, George Davis

### January 22, 1859

The Bentley family was here to see you today. Get well. You are a hero!

### January 23, 1859

I heard tell of how you walked across the river to the States. You are a brave young man! Your friend, Mr. Osborne

### January 27, 1859

Glad to see you sitting up in bed. Your friends, Mr. and Mrs. McCurdy

### January 30, 1859

We are praying for you, Corey. Reverend and Mrs. Binga

**February 2, 1859**

This is a note in the diary of Corey Birdsong from his teacher, Mr. John Alexander. You are a courageous fellow! Here are some spelling words.

COURAGE
COMPANION
FIERCE
INDEPENDENT
DETERMINATION
VICTORY
LOYALTY

**February 14, 1859**

At last I am able to write in my diary again! I was sick for such a long time. I slept and slept. I became quite thin. Many friends came to see me. Mama asked them to write in my diary. When I read what they wrote I was happy. But I am most happy that Mingo is in Canada. He lost two of his toes. But other than that, my old friend is fine.

## February 16, 1859

When Pierre told me about the box that day, I was certain that it had something to do with Mingo. When I heard that Mr. Peche had walked across the frozen river to fetch the letters, I had an idea. I would walk across the river, too. I would see about that box. I could not wait for Daddy and Mama to come home.

Pierre took me to town on his mule. I stepped onto the ice and began to walk. I walked to Bois Blanc. From the island I walked across the river at the narrowest part. The box was waiting for me on the shore. It had my name on it. There were people standing in the cold. I was afraid of the slave catchers. But no one paid me any mind.


## Same Day, Later On

I had an ax. I opened the box. Mingo was inside asleep. I woke him.

By then it was dark. But I could see the lighthouse on Bois Blanc. Mingo and I walked back across as far as the island. The river held us.

The lighthouse keeper took us the rest of the way. He had a lantern.

Mama and Daddy were on the shore, looking for me. I was so happy to see them! They put Mingo and me in a wagon and took us home.

Mama say God's eye was surely on me.

## February 18, 1859

Corey Birdsong told me to write this in his book. He tells what letters to write. Then I can write all these words.

I am Mingo. I ran away to Ohio. The Underground Railroad put me in a box. They put Corey's name on the box. They put the box on the boat. But someone took the box off. Then Corey found me.

## February 28, 1859

Today Mingo and I walked to the creek. It still hurts Mingo to walk at times, because of what happened to his toes. I showed Mingo my swan. His wing is all well, but he hasn't flown away.

**March 1, 1859**

I have gone back to school. Mingo goes to school also. We walk slowly. Daddy has found Mingo a large pair of soft boots. They once belonged to Reverend Binga.

Daddy and Mama are eager to plant. After the last frost we will plant carrots and squash and 'taters. We will plant peanuts. We will put in corn and onions. Daddy says that Mama will have chickens. We will save our money for a cow.

Star will not keep still. She is crawling everywhere!


**March 6, 1859**

Today Gwen and the Thurman family came to supper at our house. Gwen was wearing a blue ribbon. I did the bluebird song for her.

Mingo's foot does not trouble him much. He will work in the quarry with Mr. Thurman on Saturdays.

**March 12, 1859**

The sky was white with swans this morning. They are coming up from the South. Their wings made a whistling sound. Mingo and I walked to the creek. Swan was gone.

**March 15, 1859**

After church today we said farewell to Mr. Osborne. He is going to be with John Brown. He will fight against slavery. We hope that Mr. Osborne comes back safely.

## March 17, 1859

Mama has finished her quilt. She showed it to Mrs. Bentley. It is red and blue and white and brown. The pattern is geese flying north. Mrs. Bentley admired it. She said that Mama's quilt is too good to use. She should save it to show off at the Emancipation Celebration this summer. Mama was proud of that. But Mama say her quilt is to use, it isn't for show. So she laid it across the bed for me and Mingo.

## March 23, 1859

Tonight my family stood outside and looked at the stars. We saw the drinkin' gourd, which helped guide us north. Then we talked of the old days.

We talked about Aunt Queen. We talked about Charles. Mingo say that Charles ran away long ago. Aunt Queen is still on the Hart place. She thinks that her legs will give out on her if she tries to run away.

Someday there will be no more running for any of us, Daddy say. That is my greatest wish. I want freedom for all of our people.

**March 25, 1859**

Someday I will be a teacher.

# Life in America and Canada
# in 1858

# Historical Note

In the United States during the 1850s, many African Americans lived a life of bondage. Some made daring escapes, seeking their freedom. They journeyed north to free states such as Ohio, traveling through the woods at night guided by the stars, while dogs and "slave catchers" chased

*Slave catchers.*

them. They hid out in caves. They escaped by wearing disguises or stowing away on boats and trains. Some, like Henry "Box" Brown, had friends hide them in packing crates with airholes and ship them away to free places! These runaways often had help from a group of abolitionists who became known as the Underground Railroad.

Underground Railroad "conductors" hid the fugitives in barns and cellars. They gave them food and transported them in wagons with false bottoms. Or they sent them on their way after a good night's lodging to the next safe place or "station." Under the Fugitive Slave Law of 1850, runaways who reached free Northern states could be returned to the South to a life of slavery if they were caught. So, for some people their final destination was Canada. In fact, Canadian border towns became chief stations on the Underground Railroad. Boat captains who were conductors ferried fugitives across the Great Lakes. Some arrivals in Amherstburg, Canada, had even dared to swim for their freedom, crossing the Detroit River where it was most narrow.

Slavery was abolished in Canada in 1793. The first wave of African-American refugees arrived between 1817 and 1822. By the 1850s, the black community in Canada was thriving. African Canadians had their own churches and schools. Through hard work, they had come to own farms and businesses.

*African-Canadian church in Dresden, Canada.*

Among them were carpenters, blacksmiths, seamstresses, bakers, barbers, preachers, and teachers. A woman of color named Mary Ann Shadd Cary owned a newspaper called the *Provincial Freeman*. Instead of working for slave owners, the former runaways and their descendants worked for a wage they could save or spend on themselves and their families. For those who had lived part of their lives deprived of freedom, Canada truly must have seemed like the "Promised Land."

As promising as their new home was, however, the African Canadians did not forget their old one. Many of them had left family members and friends behind in the United States. They became active abolitionists; some even became conductors on the Underground Railroad, crossing back into the States to help with rescues. Others dedicated themselves to helping new refugees settle in when they

*John Brown.*

arrived. African Canadians such as Osborne
Anderson joined John Brown in his raid on
Harpers Ferry in 1859. During the American
Civil War, many African Canadians would
join the Union Army. One of these was a
surgeon named Anderson Ruffin Abbott.

*Dr. Anderson Ruffin Abbott.*

Dr. Abbott was the son of a free man of color who had been born in Virginia. He became one of eight black surgeons to serve in the Union Army. After President Abraham Lincoln was assassinated, Mrs. Lincoln presented Dr. Abbott with a shawl that President Lincoln had worn on his way to his inauguration.

Every summer, towns like Amherstburg celebrate Emancipation Day. The celebration marks the beginning of freedom for blacks in Canada. But countless African Canadians can trace their roots to the United States. They are descendants of those refugees who crossed the border seeking freedom.

# About the Author

Sharon Dennis Wyeth is the author of *My America: Freedom's Wings*, *A Piece of Heaven*, *Once on This River*, and *Something Beautiful*, a Children's Book Council Notable Book in the Field of Social Studies. She graduated from Harvard University and lives in Montclair, New Jersey, with her husband and daughter.

"Writing about Corey's escape on the Underground Railroad in *Freedom's Wings* was so exciting that I wasn't sure how much I would enjoy writing Corey's second diary. After visiting Amherstburg, Ontario, however, and hearing the stories of the industrious and successful lives black refugees forged in Canada,

I was eager to write *Flying Free*. I loved imagining Corey's excitement in coming to a new land and going to school for the very first time. How wonderful it felt to depict the joy and relief his family would have experienced having reached their goal of freedom!

"Someday, I hope to discover more about my own African-American ancestors. Perhaps some of them also made the daring escape to Canada."

For Lewis and Nan

# Acknowledgments

The author wishes to thank Carl Westmoreland of the National Underground Railroad Freedom Center, Kirk Miner of the Jack Miner Foundation, naturalist Mike Anderson, and the New Jersey Audubon Society Schermann-Hoffman Sanctuary. Deepest appreciation goes to curator Elise Harding-Davis, research assistant Nneka Allen, and the North American Black Historical Museum in Amherstburg, Ontario.

The stanza from "The Bluebird" by Emily H. Miller and the excerpt about Mr. Audobon and his pictures (paraphrased by the author) were found in a nineteenth-century edition of *Monroe's Fourth Reader*, published by Westcott and Thomson. *The Freedom-Seekers: Blacks in Early Canada*, by Daniel G. Hill, published in 1992 by Stoddart Publishing Company, Toronto, provided a wealth of background information. Editor Amy Griffin's perfect touch, as always, contributed greatly.

Grateful acknowledgment is made for permission to reprint the following:

Cover portrait by Glenn Harrington.

Page 91: Slave catchers, The Granger Collection, New York, NY.
Page 93: African-Canadian church, North America, Black History Museum.
Page 95: John Brown, Brown Brothers.
Page 96: Dr. Anderson Ruffin Abbott, North American Black History Museum.

# Other books in the My America series

Corey's Underground Railroad Diaries

*by Sharon Dennis Wyeth*

Book One: Freedom's Wings


Elizabeth's Jamestown Colony Diaries

*by Patricia Hermes*

Book One: Our Strange New Land

Book Two: The Starving Time


Hope's Revolutionary War Diaries

*by Kristiana Gregory*

Book One: Five Smooth Stones

Book Two: We Are Patriots

Joshua's Oregon Trail Diaries

*by Patricia Hermes*

Book One: Westward to Home


Virginia's Civil War Diaries

*by Mary Pope Osborne*

Book One: My Brother's Keeper

Book Two: After the Rain

While the events described and some of the characters in this book
may be based on actual historical events and real people,
Corey Birdsong is a fictional character, created by the author,
and his diary is a work of fiction.

Copyright © 2002 by Sharon Dennis Wyeth

Library of Congress Cataloging-in-Publication Data
Wyeth, Sharon Dennis.
Flying Free / by Sharon Dennis Wyeth.
p. cm. — (My America) (Corey's Underground Railroad diary ; bk. 2)
Summary: In 1858, nine-year-old Corey Birdsong and his family, fugitive slaves
from Kentucky, build a new life in Amherstburg, Canada, while still hoping to
help those they left behind.
ISBN 0-439-24443-9 — ISBN 0-439-36908-8 (pbk.)
1. African Americans — Juvenile fiction. [1. African Americans — Fiction. 2. Fugitive
slaves — Fiction. 3. Diaries — Fiction. 4. Amherstburg (Ont.) — Fiction.
5. Canada — History — 1841–1867 — Fiction.] I. Title. II. Series.
PZ7.W9746 Fl 2002
[Fic] — dc21      2001093848

10 9 8 7 6 5 4 3 2                                    02 03 04 05 06

The display type was set in Quercus Hard.
The text type was set in Goudy.
Photo research by Dwayne Howard
Book design by Elizabeth B. Parisi

Printed in the U.S.A.
First printing, May 2002